10/11

The Let's-Read-and-Find-Out Science book series was originated by Dr. Franklyn M. Branley, Astronomer Emeritus and former Chairman of the American Museum–Hayden Planetarium, and was formerly co-edited by him and Dr. Roma Gans, Professor Emeritus of Childhood Education, Teachers College, Columbia University. Text and illustrations for each of the books in the series are checked for accuracy by an expert in the relevant field. For more information about Let's-Read-and-Find-Out Science books, write to HarperCollins Children's Books, 10 East 53rd Street, New York, NY 10022, or visit our website at www.letsreadandfindout.com.

Sid the Science Kid: A Cavity Is a Hole in Your Tooth
© 2010 The Jim Henson Company, Inc. JIM HENSON'S mark & logo, SID THE SCIENCE KID mark & logo, characters and elements are trademarks of The Jim Henson Company. All Rights Reserved.
Manufactured in China.

Library of Congress catalog card number: 2009928952
ISBN 978-0-06-185263-3

Typography by Rick Farley
10 11 12 13 14 SCP 10 9 8 7 6 5 4 3 2 1
❖
First Edition

Jim Henson's

SID
the Science
KID

STAGE 1

A Cavity Is a Hole in Your Tooth

adapted by Jodi Huelin

Collins
An Imprint of HarperCollins Publishers

Good morning, Sid!

"Oh, hi! I have a problem with this whole teeth-brushing thing. Mom and Dad keep telling me I have to brush my teeth twice a day. Twice!"

Sid thinks brushing his teeth is a lot of work.
"I have to brush my teeth and rinse and brush my gums and
brush my tongue and then rinse again and *ahhh*!"

"I've got to know—what would happen if I *just didn't brush my teeth?*"

SID! BREAKFAST TIME!

Sid races into the kitchen.
"Breakfast!"
"Good morning, Sid!" Mom says.

Sid tells his mom he wants his favorite sugary cereal, and it's OK, but . . .

"You can eat it, but when you're finished you have to brush really well," Mom says.

But Sid has an announcement to make.

I'M TIRED OF BRUSHING MY TEETH.

EXCUSE ME?

Sid's mom and dad can't believe their ears!
"Brushing your teeth is really important," Dad says.
"Here, I'll show you why."

Sid's dad shows him just a few of the foods he can eat with strong teeth.

Carrots!

Apples!

TASTY FLAKES CEREAL

Cereal!

Sid sees his dad's point . . . sort of.

THIS SOUNDS LIKE SOMETHING TO INVESTIGATE AT SCHOOL.

Sid is excited to see his friends at school.

Gabriela, Gerald, and May are waiting for him on the playground.

Sid asks the question of the day:

"Do you like brushing your teeth?"

"I do, with my special purple toothbrush!" answers Gabriela.

Gerald shows Sid *how* he likes to brush his teeth: up and down, on an angle. "But when broccoli gets stuck in my teeth, brushing's hard," Gerald says.

May shows Sid the spot where she just lost a tooth.
"I like brushing in the empty spot so it stays clean," May says.

Is Sid the only person who doesn't think brushing is great?
Maybe Teacher Susie can help them learn more.
"Come on in, we've got a lot to learn today!" Teacher Susie sings.

The kids take their seats.

"What's on your mind today?" Teacher Susie asks.

"Why do we have to brush every day?" Sid responds.

Teacher Susie holds up a picture with some teeth on it. One tooth has a black stain–a cavity.

A CAVITY IS A HOLE IN YOUR TOOTH.

Teacher Susie explains how cavities form. "If you don't brush your teeth, bacteria can grow on the food that's left behind."

"Does it hurt to have a cavity?" May asks.

"Cavities can hurt," Teacher Susie explains. "But once the dentist repairs your tooth, it will feel better."

Teeth have lots to do. They work hard.

"They help us chew," Gerald says.

"And crunch and munch," Gabriela adds.

Sid wonders how teeth do all that work.

Teacher Susie says, "Let's go to the Super Fab Lab to investigate!"

Teacher Susie explains that the best way to see what teeth actually do, and how they work, is to look at them. She hands out little mirrors like dentists use.

The front teeth are called incisors.

Next to the incisors are the canines.

The teeth way in the back are called molars.

She brings out a tray with some food.
"Now let's explore our teeth and find out their different jobs,"
Teacher Susie says.

When you eat something soft, like a banana, you use your front–or incisor–teeth.

When you bite into something hard or crunchy, like a carrot, you use your side–or canine–teeth.

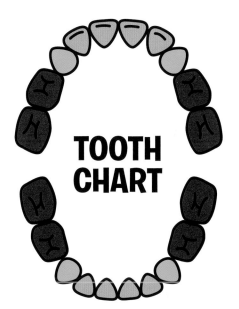

TOOTH CHART

Once you have bitten through something crunchy, you chew it up with your back–or molar–teeth.

The kids use their journals to show how teeth work.

"I ate a piece of banana using my front teeth," said Gabriela.
"Then I bit into an apple with my canine teeth. I chewed them with
my back teeth!"

Sid noted that teeth are different shapes.

"I used the mirror and saw that my front teeth are shaped like squares," Sid said. "My side teeth are pointy. And my back teeth are square, with teeny tiny bumpy hills all over them."

Those teeny tiny bumps break down food!

"Our teeth work *so* hard to chew our food," May says. Clean teeth are healthy teeth.

So *that* is why you've got to brush them every day!
"Don't worry, teeth, I'll take good care of you," says Sid.

How else can you keep your teeth healthy?
By visiting the dentist!
Sid and his friends are playing pretend–
Gerald is the dentist and May is the patient.

"Welcome to your checkup," says Dr. Gerald.

Dentists go to school–dental school–where they learn how to keep kids' teeth clean and healthy.

At the dentist's office, the dentist will clean your teeth with a special electric brush and make sure all of your teeth are strong.

Teacher Susie has a surprise for the kids. Toothbrushes!

Now Sid and his friends know how to have healthy teeth for chewing and munching and crunching.

And you do, too.

Just get a toothbrush and brush, brush, brush!

Teacher Susie showed Sid and his friends which teeth are used to chew different types of foods. Here are some more examples.

Incisor (front) teeth are thin and sharp so that they can slice into food like:

Banana

Watermelon

Cheese

Hamburger

Molar (back) teeth have ridges (or bumps) so that they can grind down food. Some cut up or bite-sized foods can be popped into your mouth directly to the molars for breaking down.

Raisins

Nuts

Grapes

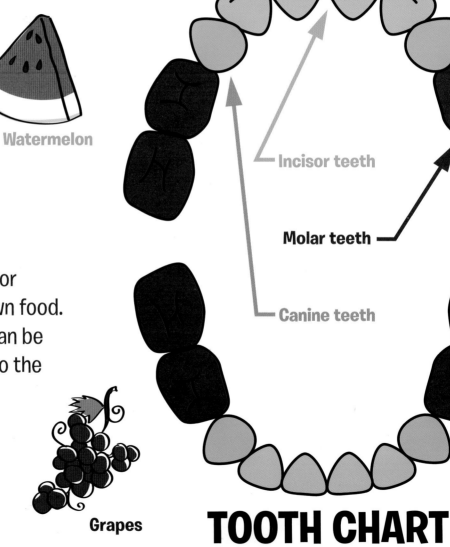

Incisor teeth

Molar teeth

Canine teeth

TOOTH CHART

Canine (side) teeth are pointy and narrow so that they can grip food like:

Carrot

Pickle

Nutty Chocolate Bar

Pretzel Stick

Celery

Fun Facts

Kids have twenty teeth.
They are called baby teeth.
Around age six, baby teeth start to fall out.

Adults have thirty-two teeth.

You know how the inside of your mouth is always kind of wet?
That wet stuff is called saliva. It helps break down the chewed-up food so that you can swallow it.

Brushing your teeth at least twice daily
(in the morning and before you go to sleep), and visiting the dentist twice yearly are the best ways to keep your teeth clean.

Sid the Science Kid's Tips for Toothbrushing:

- Squeeze a small amount of fluoride toothpaste onto a soft-bristled toothbrush.
- Starting with the outside surface of the last top tooth, place your toothbrush at the spot where the tooth meets the gum.
- Angle your toothbrush at forty-five degrees.
- Gently, using short back-and-forth brushing motions, wiggle the toothbrush ten times.
- Move to the next two teeth and repeat. Continue until all of the outside surfaces are clean, top and bottom.
- Now clean the inside of your teeth in the same way.
- Clean your front teeth, tilting the toothbrush vertically and sweeping it up and down.
- Brush your tongue to remove any bacteria that might cause bad breath.
- Spit out all of the toothpaste and rinse with water.
- Give yourself a big smile in the mirror. You just brushed your teeth!

Ask your dentist for help with toothbrushing—and flossing, too!